Freddie The Fir
The Last Christmas Tree
Jeanne Troiano

Illustrations By:
Joel Ray Pellerin

To order additional copies of this book, contact:
Xlibris LLC
1-888-795-4274
www.Xlibris.com
Orders@Xlibris.com

For my sons, Stephen, Glen, and Jason, who were the inspiration for Freddie and to my grandchildren, Danielle, Michael, Timothy, Jennifer, David, and Catherine, whose encouragement and support brought this work to life.

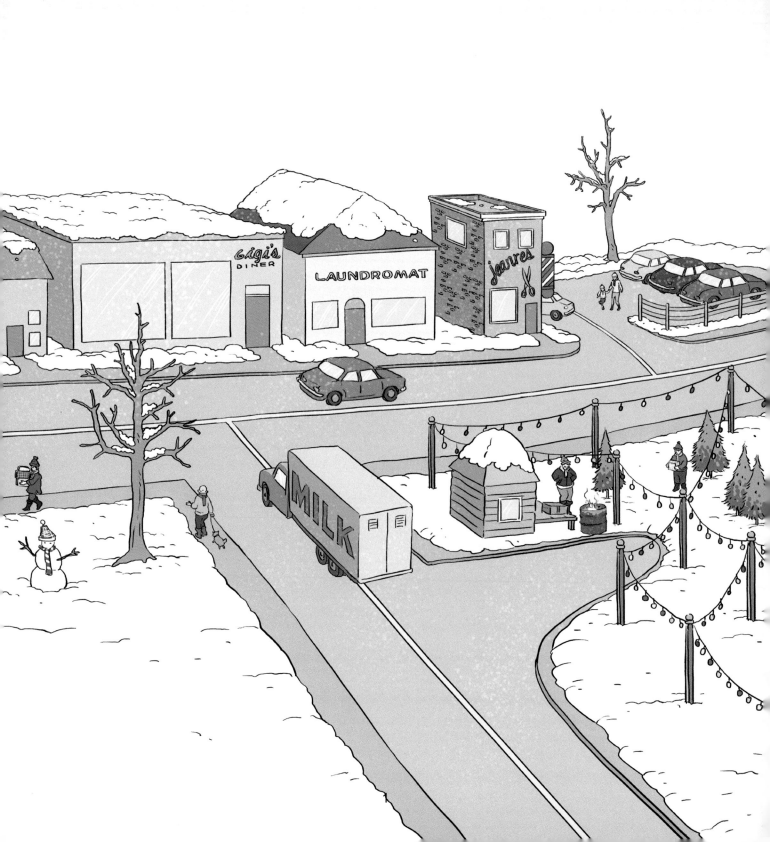

Christmas was very, very near. The children's letters to Santa were mailed, the gifts were wrapped, and all over town, the stores were beginning to quiet down. Last-minute shoppers were racing home, arms full of bundles. On the corner lot where they sold Christmas trees, some people were tying theirs on the tops of their cars and going home to decorate it before midnight. Tonight was Christmas Eve!

People didn't pay much attention to a few trees that stood around in the back of the lot unsold. Bella the Balsam, Scotty the Scotch Pine, Freddie the Fir, and a few others were standing in the round pieces of pipe that Mr. Troy, the owner, used to hold them upright. A few stragglers walked anxiously around and made their choices. A man and his wife stopped in front of Bella the Balsam, looking at her from all sides. Bella wished very hard that they would pick her. The man wasn't too sure. He glanced over at Scotty, the Scotch Pine.

Oh boy, Scotty thought, *this is it, I'm going.*

"Hey," Freddie whispered, "I'm over here. C'mon, take a look at me."

Of course, the man couldn't hear the trees. He thought for a while, *I'd like the pine. It looks good, nice and full, and it won't need a lot of ornaments.* He remembered with a smile the tree last year. His wife walked back to Bella the Balsam, who was standing right next to Freddie the Fir.

"We had a pine last year," she said. "Let's get this balsam, OK?"

Oh boy, Freddie thought. *I was hoping they would pick me.*

Bella waved her branches as they carried her past her friends. "Goodbye, Scotty. Goodbye, Freddie. Hope you get picked soon."

The owner, Mr. Troy, spun a net around Bella with a machine that whirred, he whistled as he worked. And just like that, Bella was gone.

People were leaving the lot. Some had trees, some had loose branches for making wreaths and decorations. Scotty the Scotch Pine and Freddie the Fir were still waiting.

"Aye, laddie, relax. We have time," Scotty told Freddie.

"*No*, we don't, Scotty," Freddie answered his friend. "It's late, and I'm afraid there aren't many people looking over here at us."

But just as he finished saying that, a boy and a girl came running toward Scotty and Freddie. They looked excitedly at both trees. Scotty puffed himself up. He was getting a little anxious too. The children looked at Scotty with big smiles.

Oh no, Freddie thought, *not again*.

The children ran to their mother. They wanted Scotty.

"I told you, children, this year, you could pick out the tree, so if you agree on the pine, you got it."

"Now wait a minute," Freddie the Fir said. "Look at me! You didn't even look at me!"

But the children can't hear Freddie. Again, the whir of the machine and Scotty was tied and ready to go to his new home.

"So long, laddie," Scotty said as they carried him past Freddie and put him in a van.

"Goodbye, Scotty," Freddie said in a sad whisper.

"Merry Christmas!" the little boy and girl said to Mr. Troy.

"Merry Christmas back to ya," he answered waving his hand as their car drove off.

Suddenly, Freddie the Fir was alone. The other trees were gone. All gone.

How could this be? thought Freddie. *I remember when we were all in the woods. The trucks would come and load the trees just before Thanksgiving.*

So many times Freddie would hear the trucks leaving and knew they were going to the towns and cities to make someone happy at Christmas. But Freddie was too small back then. He had to wait, and wait and wait. One Christmas then another and another, and finally, this time, when the men came for the trees, he, Freddie the Fir, was the first tree taken for the trip.

How could I be the last tree on this lot? I was the first *tree picked!* As Freddie thought about this, he was saddened, and his branches began to droop a little. He saw no one else on the lot. All the other trees, his friends Bella and Scotty, were gone. No more people were walking through. Freddie watched as Mr. Troy put out the fire in the metal drum he used to warm his hands during the long cold hours he worked. He felt snowflakes on his nose.

"Well," Mr. Troy said to himself, "might as well go home. Nothing left but that one fir tree. I'll get rid of it after Christmas."

"Get rid of! Get rid of!" Freddie cried. "Hey, mister, that's me you're talking about, and I don't want to be rid of . . . I . . . I . . . WAIT, mister!" Panic gripped Freddie. "Where are you going? Don't go, please don't go. If you leave now, no one will be able to pick me. Wait a little longer. Please. Hey!" Then a little louder. "HEY!" But Mr. Troy kept on walking. No matter how loudly Freddie shouted, Mr. Troy could never hear him.

Mr. Troy looked all around. The fire was out. Nothing left to do but shut the lights. He pulled a switch by the fence, and all the rows of lights over the lot went out.

Wow, Freddie thought. *It's dark. It's scary. No other trees around to talk to. I never noticed how dark it was when all the other trees were here.* He realized something else. *I'm all alone. Really alone. I'm the last Christmas tree on the lot, in the whole world. Me, Freddie the Fir, the last Christmas tree.*

Slowly, searchingly, Freddie looked around. Mr. Troy was gone. The gate was closed, no one was on the street. Everything was very quiet. The wind blowing and the snow falling were the only things Freddie felt moving. He drooped some more. The snow always tickled the trees when it touched the branches, and the trees always tingled. But not this time. Not tonight.

"Christmas Eve and I'm all alone. It would have been better if I was still in the woods." Freddie sighed. He wished it would snow hard and fast and cover him completely. That way, no one could see him and know he was still there.

Off in the distance, Freddie heard the sound of tires crunching on the new-fallen snow. Looking up, he saw the headlights of a car coming toward the lot. It slowly pulled up right in front of Freddie. Someone was looking into the lot. A man was moving his head side to side, trying to see something. Freddie was so excited he wanted to do something to attract the man. He moved some of his branches, hoping the man in the car would notice.

"Look, I'm right here." He motioned shaking the longest branches. "Over here, over here!" But it was no use. No matter how much he moved, the man couldn't see Freddie. He was too far away.

"Footsteps," Freddie said. "I hear footsteps. Someone is walking in the snow." Then he heard the voices.

"Yep, just closed. Was on my way home." It sounded l like Mr. Troy. But how could that be? He had left a while ago.

"Couldn't you just let me see it?" another voice asked Mr. Troy. "I was supposed to pick up a tree earlier, but I got so busy, I ran out of time."

"Come on," Freddie said. "Let him in. Let him look. It won't take long. Don't let me be here on Christmas. It's my last chance."

"Well," Mr. Troy finally said, "make it quick. I wanna go home too. Would have been gone if my dog hadn't run off. I had to wait for him to get back."

"Oh *wow*. Thank you, dog," Freddie said. "Thank you."

The man got out of the car. "This won't take long," he said.

The old man opened the gate. They walked right to Freddie. "Here it is. Last one on the lot." He pointed at Freddie. "Not much of a choice." He laughed. "It needs work, but it is *big*."

"Let's see," the other man said, and as he did, Freddie tried with all his might to lift his branches.

Got to look good, he thought. "Up, up, branches," he said. "You in the back, get up. You big one over there, move, *move*, cover up that little broken branch on the bottom. Good. That's better. Later, we—"

Just then, Mr. Troy grabbed Freddie and turned him around. "HEY!" Freddie said. "Take it easy. Turn me slower. Let him get a good look."

The two men didn't talk for a while. "You want it?" Mr. Troy asked the other man. "It's getting late, and I'd like to get going."

Give him time, Freddie thought. *Don't chase him away before he gets a chance to think it over.*

"OK, tie it up. I've got to be going myself."

Freddie was so happy. He too was going home with someone for Christmas. "All the other trees and Bella the Balsam, Scotty the Scotch Pine, and now *me*."

It was now Freddie's turn to be tied. The machine spun around and around, and he could feel his branches pressed in real close to him for the trip. Mr. Troy helped the man with the tree. They put Freddie in the back of a station wagon.

"OUCH! Watch my branches," Freddie said. "Don't break anything *now*."

The men said good night and wished each other a Merry Christmas. Freddie lay in the back of the wagon. He was happy, even happier than when the men in the woods took him for the trip in the lot. He heard the tires crunching in the snow as the wagon headed down the road. After a while, the wagon stopped. A door opened, and he heard more voices.

"This must be where he lives. That means . . . I'm home!" Freddie was so excited, he couldn't wait to get inside.

The back door of the station wagon opened, and two men pulled Freddie out. "Take it easy," Freddie said. "Lift, lift, don't drag me. You'll snap a branch."

And almost as though they could actually hear Freddie, they did lift him to get him out. "That's better." He smiled, and before he knew it—WHOOSH!—they stood him up.

"Not bad," the other voice said.

"You wait," Freddie promised. "I'm gonna be the best Christmas tree you ever had. You'll see."

"Let's get it in and get started," said the man who brought Freddie home.

After a short walk from where the car was parked, Freddie was inside. "This is the first time I've ever been inside any place in my entire life. Boy is this place big!" he said to himself.

They walked Freddie down a long corridor and into another room. "Here," another voice said, "put him in the stand and let's get started."

Everyone was fussing over Freddie, and he was enjoying all the attention. Someone put lights on him, and others were busy with ornaments and then the tinsel, and something they called garland made Freddie want to move—it tickled his branches. He stood up so tall. He thought his branches were full of ornaments and lights and were just a little bit heavy, but he kept his branches up.

"I'm gonna be the best tree," Freddie said. "Even if I'm tired, I'm not going to droop, not even a little. I'll stand straight and tall, for this is my Christmas too."

Everyone stood back and looked at the top. "Oh no, I suppose it broke when they were taking me out of the wagon."

He watched as the men brought over a ladder. A lady climbed the ladder. Everyone was watching her. She placed something on top.

What is that? Freddie wondered.

Soon, all the people were smiling and saying, "Now it looks like a Christmas tree."

The packages, all wrapped with pretty ribbons, were placed under the tree. Trucks, cars, paint sets, games, dolls, spacemen, all kinds of toys were added with loving care. Freddie was happy as he thought, *If only I could see me. Everyone else can see me.* He carefully looked down so as not to disturb anything on his branches, and all he saw was the tops of decorated branches and the packages on the floor. He looked up just as carefully and saw the bottoms of the branches and something shining all the way up on top. It got very quiet.

"That's it," someone said. "Let's go home. We have to be back early. Tomorrow's Christmas."

Tomorrow's Christmas, Freddie thought. *How wonderful tomorrow's Christmas! There will be people and children, and I have a place to be. Even if I can't see me, other people will, and that's OK.*

The last people walked out of the room. They looked back once, shut off the light, and left. The doors closed, and Freddie was alone. Again. But this time, he wasn't scared. This time was different. He was not alone like he was on the lot, when all the other trees were picked and he wasn't, when he was frightened, abandoned, and alone. This was different. This time he knew that, in a while, he'd be surrounded by happy, cheerful children and grown-ups. Freddie knew he'd better rest, but he couldn't. He was too excited, too happy. He was going to spend this night, Christmas Eve, making sure his branches were all just right.

"Gotta get that little one up a little more and keep my top straight. Oh boy, that garland tickles." He giggled at himself.

Christmas morning. A lady in green scrubs surprised Freddie when she came into the room by herself. "Hey!" Freddie was alarmed as he looked past her to see that she was alone. "Where are the children? There are supposed to be children."

The lady walked right over to Freddie, looked at him from top to bottom, and said, "Tree, you've got a big job to do here. You see, the children that will be coming in here in a minute are in the hospital. Now it's bad enough being sick, but being sick and away from home . . . that's no fun".

She stopped talking and moved toward Freddie. She pointed a finger at him and continued, "Well, you'll just make it a little nicer for them." She leaned over and reached her hand right in between the branches. CLICK.

Freddie was startled. Then when he saw her smile, he realized what the "click" was. "Oh lights," Freddie said. "Such beautiful lights—red, green, blue, yellow, white, and . . ."

As he was looking at the lights, the doors opened, and the children rushed into the room. Some of them were smiling as they came in, others were laughing, and some moved silently with their eyes staring in wonder at this beautiful tree. Some were walking, the little ones were being carried, and still others were in wheelchairs. Freddie heard the children exclaim, "Wow, look at that tree!"

When he heard all the *oohs* and *aahs*, "I'm so happy," Freddie the Fir said to himself. "Look at their faces, not a sad one in the room."

Just then, he heard the tinkling of bells and a chubby man in a red suit came into the room. The children screamed, "SANTA CLAUS! SANTA CLAUS!" and Santa Claus waved to each child and each grown-up and said, "Ho! Ho! Ho! Merry Christmas, Merry Christmas!"

Santa came right over to Freddie and sat down on a big high-backed chair. "Oh," Freddie said. "Look at this. Me and Santa side by side. How lucky I really am!"

As the presents were being given out by Santa, more people came into the room, and together, they sang Christmas carols. And Freddie still wasn't tired. Freddie puffed himself way, way up to look out at the people. The children were holding their gifts from Santa. He could see paint sets and a truck and dolls and a football and . . . and . . .

As he looked up to see more, he said, "What's that?" Freddie couldn't believe it. As he looked out at the people, he said, "NO!" and he looked again. Could it be? Could it really be? Freddie looked once more. He didn't notice it last night in the dark, but now he was sure. Yes. Yes. He would have screamed if he knew how.

"That's ME!"

For on the wall across the room was a big mirror, and Freddie could see himself. "I'm beautiful," Freddie said. He smiled as he saw all the shiny tinsel and that funny tickling garland.

"Everything is so beautiful. I never dreamed I'd see me all decorated." As he looked into the mirror, he looked up, way up on top, and for the first time, he saw it—the star . . . HIS STAR.

Freddie the Fir had his own star, and he wasn't alone. All the people and the children all helped make Freddie the Fir the last Christmas tree, the HAPPIEST Christmas tree.

HOW DO YOU SEE FREDDIE?

COLOR FREDDIE THE WAY YOU SEE HIM